PLANET OMAR

UNEXPECTED SUPER SPY

ZANIB MIAN
ILLUSTRATED BY
NASAYA MAFARIDIK

PLANET OMAR

UNEXPECTED SUPER SPY

HODDER CHILDREN'S BOOKS

First published in Great Britain in 2020 by Hodder and Stoughton

5 7 9 10 8 6 4

Text copyright © Zanib Mian, 2020
Illustrations copyright © Nasaya Mafaridik, 2020

The moral rights of the author and illustrator have been asserted.

A CIP catalogue record for this book
is available from the British Library.

ISBN 978 1 444 95127 1

Printed and bound in Great Britain by
Clays Ltd, Elcograf S.p.A.

The paper and board used in this book
are made from wood from responsible sources.

Hodder Children's Books
An imprint of
Hachette Children's Group
Part of Hodder & Stoughton
Carmelite House
50 Victoria Embankment
London, EC4Y 0DZ

An Hachette UK Company
www.hachette.co.uk

www.hachettechildrens.co.uk

This book is dedicated to all the children

who do something for someone else,

just to put a smile on their face.

DANIEL

used to bully me and Charlie, but now we are friends

his sister Suzy has to go to the hospital a lot, which means he's on his best behaviour at home

sometimes his worst behaviour comes out at school

will surprise you with his hobbies

CHAPTER 1

RASSSHHH!

That was the sound of my ceramic Stormtrooper money box breaking into 100 pieces. I had turned it upside down and tapped it against the metal leg of my desk because I thought that was a good idea for getting the money out. It wasn't. But at least my money was there and it looked like **A LOT**.

I needed to get it out to buy this really cool Laser Nerf Blaster I saw on TV. I had accidentally

5

broken my last one the time we had a Nerf

battle at my cousin Reza's house. I'd been

imagining that everyone was turning into

MAN-EATING GIANTS WITH
GREEN WARTS ALL OVER
THEIR FACES and got a bit carried

away. That's the best part – pretending you're

running away from something way scarier than

your cousins and friends.

While I was counting my riches, Maryam

came in and said,

'YOU'RE SUCH
    AN IDIOT. You know there is a little

rubbery bit at the bottom you can just open the

thing with?'

'I know,' I said. I actually didn't know, so

I felt kind of stupid and I tried really hard to

think of something smart to say, but, in the meantime, Maryam tried to sit on my wheelie chair, which wheeled itself away from her with a mind of its own. She completely missed the seat and hit the floor, and we both almost wet ourselves laughing.

She disappeared back to her room after that, leaving me to add up all my coins and notes. In total I had £42.53. Super cool – that had to

be enough to buy the Nerf Blaster! I borrowed
Mum's phone and rang my best friend Charlie
just to tell him.

'WHOA!
HOW DID YOU
GET THAT MUCH?' he said.

'I put all the money I got for Eid and all
the money I got for my birthday in there. Dad
said it would be worth the wait for something
awesome if I saved up.'

'Aw, man, that's cool. I spend my money the
minute I get it.'

I told Charlie that I used to do that too, but
then I imagined that if I saved enough money,
one day I could pay people to let me drive even
though I'm only a kid. And maybe I would have

enough money to buy a Ferrari too, because they're only like £150,000, which surely couldn't take that long to save up.

Mum called up the stairs that it was time to get off the phone and put my shoes on to go to the mosque. But she said it really nicely and she even called me sweetie, so I didn't think it was that urgent and I carried on chatting to Charlie and daydreaming about my Ferrari. Charlie was daydreaming too because I said I'd pay people to let him drive as well.

Then Mum came and blew my ears off.

'I SAID PUT YOUR SHOES ON!'

Yikes!

'Bye, Charlie.'

Our mosque trips had become even more fun since Dad started coming with us. He changed things around so that he doesn't have to go to the lab on Saturdays any more, which means more cool things can happen on weekends now. He even took me go-karting recently, which was the **best saturday ever!**

Gulp. I couldn't find my left shoe and Mum was going to lose it if I didn't get this done in fifteen milliseconds . . . Yes! I saw it on top of the sofa and grabbed it while Dad stood over me with a face like that emoji whose lips are just a very straight line. But when I went to put it on, I saw that it had been treated to a dose of my little brother Esa's

slime in a Bucket.

I didn't dare complain or look for other shoes, so I shoved my foot in. It was DISGUSTING. Like I was stepping on a

GAZILLION ZOMBIE EYEBALLS

Ewwwwwhwww.

I squidged and SQUIRTED my way to the

Peanut (that's our car) and jumped in.

At the mosque, when we were all praying,

Esa sat on my head and made me laugh. I had

to control myself before it turned into a full-

on giggle fit, so I imagined that there was a

SUPERVILLAIN holding me in a

head-lock and if I laughed out loud, he would

blow up the whole entire universe, but if I kept

quiet as a mouse, he would release me and the

universe would be safe . . .

PHEW, I managed it. I was pretty

pleased with myself, especially when Dad

turned and winked at me when the prayer was

finished. I know why he did it. To show me that

he saw Esa on my head and that he was proud of how I handled it. Also because he was in a good mood. He's always in a good mood at the mosque, and he has a different sort of smile on his face while we're there. Maybe it's a **Secret Smile** that's only for Allah or something. I think he's really glad we found such a great mosque close to our new house. All the others Mum made us try out when we first moved are ages away. Dad says he's really happy that it has the kind of vibes that make him feel closer to Allah. Mum and Dad like those kinds of vibes and they reckon you don't get them in every mosque. Everyone is really nice to each other and it's quiet and light comes streaming in through the windows on sunshiny days.

CHAPTER 2

On Monday, at school, I rolled in with an imaginary Nerf Blaster in my arms and targeted my best friend Charlie.

He gave me the very same toothy grin that made me like him when I moved to this school recently. Then he pulled out his own from under the table (imaginary too, of course) and pretended to blast me right back.

I think his imagination has been getting

stronger since we became friends, like a muscle

does when you lift up weights all day long.

When Daniel saw us, he giggled and punched

me on the arm. Don't worry, it

was one of those FRIENDLY ones

that don't hurt at all. Daniel is our friend now.

He doesn't actually bully anyone any more, not even Charlie, who used to be his favourite subject of all things horrid. There's no way we'd be friends with a bully, but it turns out Daniel had reasons for being so naughty at school, and now he has us as friends to hang out with, he's

TOTALLY DIFFERENT.

'It's a Laser Nerf Blaster,' I announced. 'Imaginary for now, but I'm going to get a real one with my pocket money.'

'Oh cool!' said Daniel. 'I want one.'

'Me too!' chipped in Charlie.

'Let's all get them and have an

EPIC NERF BATTLE.

We can all pretend to be spies, like James Bond chasing down an evil villain,' Daniel said excitedly.

OH YEAAAAH!

Charlie and I said at the same time. We often say things at the same time, which is super funny and sometimes super freaky.

'Have you got enough pocket money?' I asked.

'No, but my mum said she was going to

buy me something for, ermmm . . .' Daniel sheepishly scratched the back of his head instead of finishing his sentence.

'For what?'

Charlie and I did it AGAIN. Same words, same time. Same wanting to know what Daniel was getting treated for.

'Errrm . . .'

'For washing your dad's car?' I guessed.

'For tidying your room?' Charlie guessed.

Daniel did some more sheepish head scratching.

I tried another guess. 'For getting 10/10 in your spelling test?'

'No . . . no . . . erm . . . actually for settling so much better at school and making such good friends.'

Daniel air-quoted as he blushed bright red.

Charlie and I both jumped onto Daniel to give him a **hug**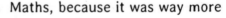. I think he was blushing because he's not always 100% sure that we like him as our friend, but we super definitely do. We keep finding so many things that we like to do together – like the Nerf Blasters!

We couldn't help but talk about it all during Maths, because it was way more

 exciting than learning about what a denominator was and how we could think about a pizza in fractions.

The only thing I think when I see a pizza is how quick I can get it into my mouth. Mrs Hutchinson was very excited about fractions. I could tell because her curly hair

was all big and sproingy. That's what I like about Mrs Hutchinson – she thinks everything is entertaining.

'I CANNOT WAIT for the Nerf battle. It's going to be crazy fun!' I whispered.

And Charlie whispered, 'I knowwwwww. I just have to think of a way to convince my parents to buy me one too.'

'You do know that both of you whisper as loud as you talk?' pointed out Daniel.

He was right, because Mrs Hutchinson came over, attempting to put her cross face on, and said, 'Stop chatting and tell me how much pizza is on the board, boys.'

'Not enough for me,' said Daniel.

AND WE ALL EXPLODED WITH LAUGHTER.

We had to clap our hands over our mouths quickly before Mrs Hutchinson got upset.

Then Charlie said, 'One-sixth, miss,' with his toothy grin.

PHEW, Mrs Hutchinson was pleased enough with us, even with all our giggling.

I couldn't wait to get home and ask Mum and Dad if they were OK with us having a big Nerf showdown at home and would they please order pizza that day? Maybe I could promise to talk about the pizza as fractions, like Mrs Hutchinson was doing, then they'd be up for it for sure,

SO CHEESY

because they are about brainy stuff like that.

They say it's because they're scientists, but I

think they're scientists *because* they like brainy

stuff. It's like the

chicken and egg situation.

CHAPTER 3

Mum picked me up by foot. WHOA, did
you just imagine her with a
SUPER-HUGE
FOOT, lifting me up by my collar? I
did. But that's not what I meant. I meant that
she didn't bring her car. She walked. This is her
new thing. Walking as much as we can to help
the environment and be fit like Batman. It takes
13 minutes or 467 steps to get home. I counted
it the first time Mum made us walk and that

number is *almost* correct. It would be more correct if Esa hadn't interrupted my counting by singing 'Old MacDonald had a Farm' at the top of his voice.

Today, instead of counting steps or imagining that if I stepped on a crack in the pavement it would cause an earthquake like I sometimes do, I asked Mum about the Nerf battle.

'Please, Mum, you're so pretty'

I grinned.

'Cheeky!' said Mum. 'Funny how you only tell me that when you want something . . .'

I laughed and switched on my

pester-power puppy-dog eyes.

'OK, fine. As long you don't use tomato paste as monster gore like you did with Reza.'

'I wouldn't dream of it!' I said. But my brain was bursting at the memory of how FUN that had been.

'And when did you say you wanted to do it?' She looked a bit sad now. 'I don't think it could be this weekend because we have to go to a meeting at the mosque on Sunday. They need to talk to us about raising enough money to keep it from closing down . . . It was just announced today on the WhatsApp group.'

'WHAAAAAT?

The mosque? Our mosque?

the secret-smile mosque?'

'Secret-smile mosque?' said Mum.

'Yeah! You and Dad have secret smiles in that mosque.'

'Yes, then – the secret-smile mosque.'

I couldn't believe it. My chest felt the way it did when our budgie, Dodo, had died when we lived in the old house.

'Wait. You said they have to raise money, right? So it might not have to close down?'

'That's right. Hopefully it won't.'

i dRAGGeD mY feEt the rest of the way home.

As soon as I got in, **STAIRS** **THE** ↑ **UP** **SHOT** I

to get my cash from
its new hiding place.
The best hiding place *ever*.

It was rolled up in a green pair
of underpants and placed carefully between
my old shoes at the back of the cupboard. My
underpants were something Maryam would
never, EVER touch, no matter
how desperate she was.

I took the £42.53
downstairs and put it on
the table.

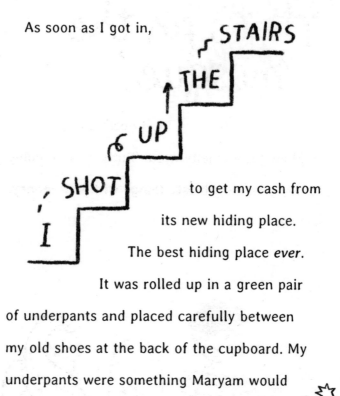

'That's for the mosque,'

I declared.

Mum got all melty-eyed. 'But you were going to buy your Nerf blasty thingy with that money, sweetie.'

'Laser Nerf Blaster. Yes, Mum. It's OK. I want the mosque to have it. Now it won't have to shut down.'

'Errrrrmmm I *think* they need a bit more than that, stupid,' said Maryam.

'Maryam!' Mum scolded. Then she came and took my chin in her hand and said, 'That is so very wonderfully kind of you, Omar.

I am very, very proud of you right now.

I think the mosque does need a whole lot more, but we will find out on Sunday just how much.'

Maryam scoffed, I guess because Mum wasn't proud of her.

'However much they need, I will get it!' I said.

AND I MEANT iT.
I
SUPER
MEANT iT.

CHAPTER 4

That night, when I closed my eyes to go to
sleep, I kept seeing a DINOSAUR,
the size of a block of flats destroying the
secret-smile mosque with one flick of his
tail and then picking up the little pieces and
putting them on his ice cream, like they were
hundreds and thousands.

I didn't want to imagine that happening to
the mosque. I shook my head and jumped out
of bed. I had the fantastic idea of playing on
my Xbox to distract myself.

BUT FIRST, I HAD TO SILENTLY SNEAK DOWNSTAIRS IN THE DARK, LIKE A BURGLAR. I TIPTOED OUT OF MY ROOM, AVOIDING THE SPOT" WHERE THE SQUEAKY" FLOORBOARD WAS. TO HELP ME CONCENTRATE I PRETENDED I WAS STEPPING OVER SECURITY LASERS ON THE STAIRS THAT WOULD SET OFF AN "ALARM"~ IF I WASN'T CAREFUL ENOUGH.

I made it! But just when I was about to buy a wicked new car in my game, Mum walked in and went nuts.

'Omar! It's a school night! And what do I see? You're up at 10:30. 10:30! TEN! THIRTY! On your Playbox!'

I knew I was in TROUBLE, but I couldn't help giggling. 'It's an Xbox, Mum. There's also such a thing as a Play Station, which I wish I had as well . . . but, erm, no Playbox.'

Dad poked his head round the door and said, 'You have two seconds to shut that off and get into bed, smarty-pants.'

'But it will take me at least seven seconds to walk upstairs to my bed.'

'Right, that's it,' said Dad and he came and picked me up and held me under his arm like you would hold a football. Just like that. That's because he's big and really strong.

We both giggled as he plunked me down onto my duvet. Dad put his finger to his lips and nodded towards little snoring Esa. 'Shh now, and get some sleep,' he whispered.

This time, when I closed my eyes, I saw

Dad's Secret Smile.

I couldn't bear the thought of him losing it. I *had* to dream up a clever way to raise more money . . .

CHAPTER 5

The next day at school, I waited till lunchtime
to tell Daniel and Charlie that I was really sorry
but I wouldn't be able to buy a Nerf Blaster
for myself any more, which meant we couldn't
have a proper Nerf battle.

I didn't want to tell them in the morning,
because Mrs Hutchinson had started the day
with an awesome biscuit-decorating session
for us. She had brought in all sorts
of toppers and sprinkles and bits of
fudge and M&M's. And, as you

know, that isn't something that teachers do very often. She said it was a lesson about 'how to prepare food', but I'm pretty sure it was mostly because she likes chocolate chips and she likes us – that's another reason why she's

the BEST TEACHER ever!

Charlie and Daniel were so happy, gobbling sweets and making biscuits with all the available toppings on them that I just kept my mouth shut about the bad news.

At lunchtime we got SMELLY

cauliflower spring rolls with 'steamed carrots',
which may as well have been steamed sloth
fingers, because they were so brown and gross.
After we had finished complaining about the
school cook and wondering how much Jamie
Oliver would charge to be the chef at our
school, I blurted out the bad news.

'I have to tell you something . . . I can't buy
a Nerf Blaster any more.'

Daniel jumped up as if his bottom had been

PRICKED BY A HEDGEHOG

and ran in circles round Charlie and me
screaming,

NOOOOOOOO!

Charlie looked at me with a smile so big I could almost see his gums. He liked it when Daniel behaved all crazy wild, as long as it wasn't against him or us, like it used to be.

'Because, Daniel . . .' I said loudly over his screaming, 'the mosque is going to close down if they don't get enough money.'

Daniel stopped suddenly with his jaw dropped and said, 'Really?'

'Yes. Super really.'

He started up again and this time Charlie and I joined in.

When our lungs screamed back at us to stop, we fell down onto the floor.

I had known Daniel would be upset, too. Ever since we got lost together on the London Underground and been chased by a not-really-zombie, Daniel has often talked about the London Central Mosque – because that's where we ended up being rescued. I think he's decided that mosques have superpowers or something. He even insisted on going to my local mosque with me once to see what it was like and whether they have halal sweets there too.

(They do. Daniel ate three packets and went home with a blue tongue.)

We made a new friend there that day, a girl called Aisha who doesn't go to our school but who likes Batman almost as much as Daniel does. That kind of nice thing often happens at the mosque, not just for kids but for grown-ups too. That's probably another reason why Dad has a secret smile there – he says that it isn't just a place for praying, it's a place where a single person becomes part of something bigger. I'm not exactly sure what he means by that, but I guess the mosque IS quite a lot

BIGGER

than a house. You couldn't fit everyone who goes there into our front room for tea and cake . . . though I bet my mum would try it if she could.

After we'd fallen down on the floor, we were all quiet for a little while. Then Daniel whispered 'no' in a very small voice.

'No,' whispered Charlie too.

'No,' I whispered.

And we decided right there that we were all going to help the mosque **together.**

CHAPTER 6

It was the first Sunday in three months that

we had to cancel our family tradition of

SCiENCE SUNDAYS,

because the meeting in the mosque was in the

morning, and Science Sunday *always* happens

in the morning. Everything at our house has its

set time and day and exactness, as if life is

ONE BIG SCiENCE EXPERIMENT.

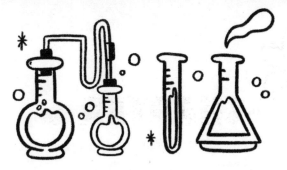

Morning is Mum and Dad's favourite time. They wake up early every morning, even in the holidays, and act as if they've drunk loads of cola, even before breakfast. Some days, Dad takes his motorbike out after his dawn prayers, so he can enjoy the empty roads. Mum always worries that he goes too fast. He always says, 'Don't worry, darling. I'm safe with it.' But I know he's not, because I've seen his face when he drives the Peanut and gets to go fast on the motorway. He looks like a kid who's just been given a lifetime's supply of Oreos. (By the way, I've *always* wanted a lifetime's supply of Oreos.

I love them and I know seventeen different ways to eat them. If Mum hadn't refused to buy them for me any more, I would know at least thirty-seven by now . . .)

Anyway, back to *this* Sunday. I couldn't wait to get stuck into the

MØN£¥ -makiNG 1ᗪEa$.

Charlie and Daniel were going to come over when we got back from the mosque, so we could start planning it out.

At the mosque meeting we found out that they needed to raise £30,000. The imam of the mosque spoke to everybody. He looked like he was sad but trying not to be.

'We've discovered an urgent issue with the mosque building.

DØN'T P∀niC!

Because it's holding for now, but it's something we need to get working on in a few weeks. The woodwork in the roof is rotting.'

The whole room full of people looked nervously up at the ceiling.

'Now, unfortunately, we don't have enough funds to pay for the work needed to fix everything, and if we can't raise it, we will have to close the mosque because it won't be safe,' the imam finished.

PHEW, I thought, that sounds kind of easy. I think I could raise £30,000 with my friends. And other people would be raising

money with their family and friends too, so

I was sure it would be OK. But the best bit

was that the imam said that if you're involved

with making a mosque, or you stop one from

shutting down, Allah will build a house for you

in *Paradise.*

whoa.

whoa.

WHOA!

I couldn't believe it. I imagined Allah

making a house for ME. And because he's

God, he would know *exactly* what my dream

house would be: it would have one room made

entirely of **trampolines**, even on the walls! One room would be a **cinema**, with all the cinema seats, so I could invite my friends. There would be **popcorn machines** in there too. There would super definitely be a games room, with all my favourite video games

and I think if I was in heaven I would even be allowed to play the games that Mum and Dad have forbidden me to play on Earth. The kitchen would be built entirely of **oreos** and the only other things available to eat and drink in there would be **PIZZA** and **milkshakes**. You could break the Oreos off the wall if you wanted, and they would just grow back. In the bedroom, the whole floor would be a water bed so you could just drop and sleep wherever you wanted. And there would be no roof, so you could see the stars and planets in the sky. Anything that you threw on the floor would magically tidy itself up into the wardrobes and shelves. Oh, and all my favourite authors would be there, all ready to read me a story. And of course Mum and Dad, because they're the best at telling stories. (Don't tell my friends, **but I still really love it when someone reads me a story.**) I guess Maryam and Esa could be there too.

I was so busy imagining my *dream house* that I didn't realise it was time to go until Maryam flicked my ear.

OUCH!

'What the **TOAD SKIN** was that for?'

'For being such a day-dreaming piece of ostrich gut!'

In case you're wondering about this strange way of insulting each other, it all began when Mum was driving and a bus pulled out when it shouldn't have, almost causing an accident, and Mum shouted,

'WHAT THE BUS ?!!'

Maryam and I looked at each other and raised our eyebrows all the way to the tops of our foreheads, because we saw what Mum did there. She swore . . . without swearing . . .

And then a couple of days later, Mum dropped a butternut squash onto her toes and screamed,

'SHHHHHH-UGAR AND TWO PANCAKES!'

That was so random that Maryam and I laughed all over the floor and we repeated it to each other and cracked up again and again. Ever since then we've been trying to come up with more and more inventive insults.

(I think I'm winning.)

HA HA HA HA

As we drove home, I was feeling excited. Not only was I going to help save the mosque, with my friends, but I was going to get my dream house for doing it!

CHAPTER 7

I ran to the door when Charlie and Daniel turned up.

Daniel was sporting a red nose because he had a cold. Dad looked horrified. He's super scared of germs, because when he gets sick, he gets really sick. He says it's a SCIENTIFIC FACT that man flu is worse than the flu that kids and women get, but Mum

says it's only because we're a lot tougher than
he is.

We went straight up to my bedroom, and I
shoved Esa's toys under his bed to make space.

'Let's brainstorm,' I said. 'Mrs Hutchinson
always makes us do that to think of ideas.'

'OK,' said Charlie.

Daniel blew his nose and nodded his head.

So I got a piece of A3 paper and my Sharpies
and wrote 'money-making ideas' in the middle.

money-making
ideas

'Right, guys. Shoot,' I said.

Leb'nade' stand, said Daniel.

'Lemonade?' I made sure.

'Yeah.'

I wrote it down.

'My uncle sells things on eBay,'

Charlie said.

'Like what?'

'Like earphones and fans and stuff like that.'

'Cool. But where can we get those from?' I

said.

'We beed bongey,' said Daniel.

Charlie and I must have looked confused,

because he tried again, 'You bow – we

dob't have aby. We're brying to *babe* bongey.'

'We do have £42.53,' I said, tuning into his blocked-nose secret code. 'I wonder how many earphones we can buy with that.'

'Or we can just *make* stuff to sell,' said Charlie.

I wrote it down.

Then I told them my idea. 'Let's hold a talent contest and charge people money to come and see it! It would be so great!'

'Cool!' said Charlie and Daniel both at the same time.

'How much should we charge them and where will we have it? Maybe I could ask my parents if we can have it here in the garden or something . . .?'

'Or maybe at the mosque?' said Charlie.

'Oh yeah. Good idea. They have a huge room.'

I wrote down **tALⱻhT CONtⱻsT** and we kept thinking.

'Do chores for bongey,' Daniel suggested.

'Like cleaning your room,' said Charlie with a cheeky grin.

We all **cracked up laughing** at the thought of asking our parents for money for cleaning our rooms.

Daniel laughed too hard before he managed

to reach for the tissue box and got snot all down his face.

'Ewwwwwww, Daniel!'

I couldn't breathe any more from laughing. Ouch, ouch, it hurt!

There's something about snot that is funny and disgusting at the same time. Like farts.

(Especially when Maryam farts after we've had curry and she pretends it isn't her...)

Anyway, by the time we were done, we had lots of ideas to get started on:

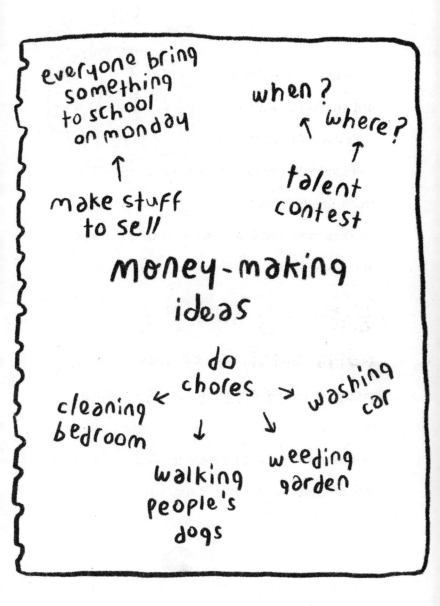

I was starving after all
that thinking! Or maybe
it was more because
Mum has been making these
funny healthy muffin things
for breakfast. They are SUPER YUCK
and SUPER DRY. Dad pretends that
he likes them so that he doesn't hurt Mum's
feelings, but once I caught him smothering one
with peanut butter when Mum wasn't looking.
Before we had gone to the mosque, I had put
my one into the pocket of my dressing gown
and just pretended I'd eaten it.

Have you ever been so hungry you felt like
you had a huge hole in your chest? I don't
understand it because it should be my tummy
that has a problem with being hungry, but for

some reason it feels more like my chest needs food to fill it up. Sometimes it feels like the hole is so big it could be a GAPING WORMHOLE, ready to suck in anything I walk past! I imagined Charlie jumping into it and ending up in some other dimension. I wondered whether he would find me and Daniel in that other dimension and what we would look like there . . . probably completely different, with green hair or something.

Luckily Dad had made his famous spaghetti bolognese as a treat since my friends were staying to eat lunch with us. He puts stuff in it that he won't tell us about, but I don't mind, because it makes it taste deeelicious. I'm OK ... as long as he's not adding

eye of newt and tongue of toad.

I guess it wasn't just me that was super hungry, because Charlie, Daniel, Maryam and even Esa shoved down the bolognese without saying a word from start to finish. When I had eaten every last bite, I looked up and realised

I was the only one who got it all over my top.

Oops!

I'm such a *messy eater* that Mum doesn't let me order spaghetti if we go out to eat. Also, it's not usually halal at restaurants.

As soon as Daniel and Charlie's parents had picked them up, Mum said, 'Right, who wants to do the Sainsbury's shopping with me?'

PING! A CHORE!

Perfect opportunity, I thought, and volunteered myself super quick.

'I'll do it with you, and pack all the bags and unpack them back at home. All for £2.50!'

'Don't be so cheeky!' said Dad. 'Since when do you get paid to help out?'

I shrugged. 'It's part of the plan to raise money for the mosque.'

That made Dad change his mind pretty quick. He said he was really proud of me and my friends for being such stars by helping to raise money. And then he said *of course* I could have £2.50 for helping with the shopping. In fact, I could have £5.00.

YESSSSS

Maryam said, 'Humph. That's so unfair,' and
stormed off to get her coat.

I like doing the grocery shopping with my
parents, because I can get stuff that they
wouldn't normally buy when they go on their
own. Sometimes I ask them if I can
pretty please have this or
that but sometimes I just
sneak it into the
busy trolley.

Esa is too
big to sit in
the trolley now
like he used to, so I also
have to put up with him
following me and picking stuff up. Once
he even dropped a jar of pasta sauce on the

floor and smashed it to smithereens, which was

soooooooooooo embarrassing.

I didn't know if I should run away and pretend I didn't know him, or stick around and help Mum deal with it.

This time, he started flinging sausages into

the trolley at the speed of Dad's motorbike.

'What are you doing, chipmunk?' said Mum.

'You can't have all those; they're not halal.'

Esa is still learning all about the food

he can't eat when he's at nursery or

restaurants and things, because of being

Muslim and needing to حلال

ONLY EAT HALAL MEAT

that has been prepared in a special way. It

can be a bit confusing for little kids, because

chicken is OK at home, because we get the

halal one, but at school it's not halal, so he doesn't always understand.

Maryam teases him for being such a **dummy.** But I feel a bit sorry for him, because he gets sad when he can't eat things he's chosen. Like after the sausages he chose some **sweets** that had gelatine in them, so he got told they weren't halal and he almost burst into tears. I helped him find some halal ones that said suitable for vegetarians on them and got a pack for myself too . . . Well, I deserved them for working so hard on this chore.

CHAPTER 8

At school on Monday, we huddled together
to share what we had brought in to sell to
kids in the playground. Charlie had made
yummy cookies at home with his mum, and
Daniel had made . . . wait for it . . .

ORIGAMI
BIRDS!

WHAAAAAT!
DANIEL CAN
DO ORIGAMI??

Charlie and I couldn't believe it! We couldn't stop quizzing him about whether he was kidding. Did his dad make them? Did he buy them? No. Apparently he'd been folding paper into things since he was six, but he'd just never shown anyone before. After that, the boiled sweets that I had found in my bedside table and shoved in my bag to sell made me feel a bit sheepish. We walked around the playground, shyly approaching kids, asking them to buy our things. Some kids just laughed and ran away. LOTS of kids told Daniel that he DID NOT make those birds and Charlie and I told them that they could bet their best friends' teeth that he did.

Sarah from our class really cheekily said,

Can I have a cookie for free?

'No,' said Daniel. 'It's 50p and no less because it's delicious.'

'Charlie would give me one for free, because

he's *kind*!' teased Sarah, with one hand on her hip.

Charlie blushed bright red and immediately handed over a free cookie. Daniel and I immediately said in unison,

After a while of walking around, we finally realised something: DUHHHHH, kids don't really bring money to school with them.

'What will we do? If we can't sell stuff to kids at school, who will we sell it to?' said Daniel.

'Maybe we can ask Mrs Hutchinson if she can talk to the parents and tell them to give their kids some money?' I suggested.

'Do you think she would listen to us?'
said Daniel, who had seen the cross side of
Mrs Hutchinson a lot when he was more of a
troublemaker.

'Definitely. She's really cool.
She always helps,' Charlie assured him.

'You ask her, Charlie,' I said, because no
matter how nice she was I still felt too shy to
ask her something like that.

'Why me?' pleaded Charlie.

''Cause you have the best smile,' I said,
quickly thinking of why we all like him so
much.

Charlie went red again and said that we
should all ask her together.

'It's a plan,' said Daniel.

'Yup,' I agreed.

So we went to find Mrs Hutchinson, who looked like she had just started her lunch, even though it was nearly the end of lunchtime. Her hair told me why: she had been very busy. Her hair couldn't hide anything. It was all over the place. Some curls looked like they had to be somewhere else, while others were desperately trying to eat her lunch.

We told her all about the plan to raise

money so that the mosque doesn't have to

close down. She looked at us as if

she was about to

BURST WITH PRIDE

and love or something. I

wondered if a human ever did actually burst

with pride and love, would balloons and

confetti and candyfloss come out of them?

'You are such generous children!' she

said. 'I'm going to help you as much as I can, but the thing is that I can't speak to parents without Mr McLeary approving it. He *is* the head teacher. I'll arrange a meeting for the three of you to tell him about your idea.'

Gulp!

Mr McLeary is the meanest meanie in the school. Everyone calls him MR MCSCARY behind his back. I have literally NEVER seen him smiling at a kid.

And now we were at his mercy . . .

CHAPTER 9

As soon as I got home from school and
swallowed a packet of crisps (and the apple
that Mum said I had to have if I wanted
the crisps) I went over to see my next-door
neighbour Mrs Rogers.

'Now there's a lovely face I haven't seen in a
while,' she said when she opened her door.

'I've been busy making plans to save the
mosque!' I told her.

'Save the mosque? Now that sounds heroic.
What are you saving it from?'

'FROM MAN-EATING ZOMBIES!'

'Oh no, when are they coming? I'll put it in my calendar,' said Mrs Rogers.

Hahahaha!

She is always unexpectedly hilarious. She surprises me every time I spend time with her, and I am not an easy kid to surprise, because my imagination has already thought of everything. It's so much better now than when we first moved in and she didn't like us.

After we finished giggling, I told her about the real situation.

'So, I actually came over to ask you if I can do some chores for you and get paid,' I said, smiling my best smile.

'Sure. You can start by washing my car.'

Mrs Rogers' car was one of the surprising things about her. My nani doesn't drive and I've never seen any other people *that old* driving, but Mrs Rogers still drives her car all the time.

She looked at me as if she was reading my thoughts, which I kept to myself because Mum and Dad say it's not polite to call people old.

'I'm as sharp as a bat you know,' she said. 'Don't be fooled by this wrinkly skin.'

And she winked.

She handed me £8.00 and I did the best I could, which must have been not too bad because Mrs Rogers seemed pleased once I was done. I had imagined

teeny-tiny

STORMTROOPERS

helping me, which made it way better, especially when my fingers were cold. ✝ Why were they teeny-tiny? Because normal-sized Stormtroopers would just be normal and that's only half as fun.

Back at home, Mum was exhausted.

'I can't wait to get off my feet!' she kept saying as she stirred the lamb korma we were having for dinner.

Hmmm, I thought. I knew how I could make her feel better and earn some money at the same time. She did everything for us all day long. She deserved a

SPA Treatment

So while she finished off her cooking, I went upstairs to get things ready.

I thought for the very best spa experience I'd have to stimulate all five senses. I got some of Mum's lotions and face creams out and put them on her bedside table. Then I went downstairs to get some cucumber. I saw a cardboard box from a parcel Mum had opened earlier with those soft white things in it for protection. Perfect. I grabbed that.

Next, I went into Maryam's room for one of her Lindor chocolates, which I know she keeps hidden in her bedside table.

She screamed at me of course.

DON'T YOU KNOW HOW TO KNOCK ?!

'Sorry.' I grinned like I was the yellow emoji
 with all the teeth showing. 'It's just that I'm trying to make Mum feel relaxed with a spa, and a chocolate treat is part of it . . . so I was wondering if I can have one of yours to give her?'

To my HUGE SURPRISE she softened up right away and threw one at me with a smile.

'Thanks!' I said.

Teenagers are super weird.

Next, I made a sign and stuck it up in the hallway.

omar's Spa

treatments available:

• face massage £2.50

• face and feet massage £3

• full-body massage £3.50

Open on Monday and Friday evenings

Well, I couldn't be stuck rubbing people's feet every day. I still wanted to play with my stuff sometimes.

'Mum! Come to my spa.'

'Your spa???'

'Yes, come, come. Quickly!'

Mum came upstairs, although she was very confused. I made her lie down on her bed and quickly plonked the cucumber slices on her eyes. I had seen that somewhere on TV.

'Eek!' Mum squealed, reaching for the cucumbers. 'What is that?'

'It's cucumber, Mum. Just be still and keep those on your eyes. I'm going to relax your tired feet now.' I put the box of white things onto the bed and stuck both her feet into it.

Mum giggled a bit.

Next, I got a dollop of face cream and started rubbing it on her face.

'Erm, wow . . .' said Mum. But she sounded like it wasn't *wow*, so I had to step things up.

'Open your mouth.'

'Ermmm, OK. What are you going to put in it?' she asked. She sounded scared.

'Just open it! And keep your eyes closed. I'm stimulating all your five senses.'

I shoved the Lindor through her hesitating lips.

She relaxed a little bit, I could tell. She likes Lindor.

Then I remembered I hadn't stimulated the

hearing sense. I cranked the
volume up and hit play on my
iPad. It was Sunflower from
the *Spider-Verse* movie.

Mum **jumped.**

'Oh. Oh . . . OK. Sorry,
I wasn't expecting that, sweetie,' she said
and pretended to be relaxed.

'I'm going to massage your feet now,' I
announced.

I tipped out some lotion. Lots of it.

'Oh, that's cold,' said Mum. But then after a
while she added, 'It does feel good, actually. I
needed that.'

FINALLY, I thought.

Ooops, I forgot the fifth sense. Smell. I ran

to the bathroom and got the air freshener. I

thought seven quick squirts should do

the job.

Mum coughed a bit and

choked out, 'Ermm, can

I go downstairs? I need

to check the curry.'

'No, you have to stay

like that for two hours,' I

explained. Well, nobody can relax

properly in ten minutes. 'Dad's home now.

I'll ask him to check it.'

Mum said, 'Ooooook . . .' and gave in.

She didn't end up staying two hours in the

end, because we had to have dinner. I was glad

anyway; I didn't realise how slow two hours

can be when you're rubbing someone's feet.

Mum gave me £10.00 instead of the £3.50 I had written on the advert for the spa. As soon as the note hit my hand, Maryam appeared from nowhere with a scowl on her face.

'Dinosaur's fart,' she said. She was referring to me. 'You think you're clever, but last night I saw you trying to open a wall to get into the bathroom.'

'Yeah, right!' I said. This was such a hilarious thought. I chuckled super loud.

But Maryam wasn't chuckling with me. She was looking at me as if she was a rhino and I was getting in the way of its waterhole.

GULP. I knew that face. She was up to something.

CHAPTER 10

Have you ever had wobbly knees?

I mean actual, literal wobbly knees. I could feel mine shaking as I stood in the line with the rest of the class waiting to go into the classroom on Tuesday morning. It was supposed to be a straight line, and it sort of was, except half the kids were doing this new dance from a computer game we all like. Even Daniel! Anyway, back to my knees. They were wobbly because it was the day we had to speak to

MR McSCARY about selling stuff to the other kids. Charlie had arrived with his glasses on all wonky, as if they were wobbly just like my knees.

We hated to remind Daniel what day it was, but we had to. As soon as we told him, Daniel stopped waving his arms around, and we all stood there not talking at all.

To make things worse we had to get through half the day first, because Mr McScary was going to meet us at lunchtime. Luckily we had some fun lessons, like Science and making up rhyming poems in Literacy. Here's mine:

Food is cool, food is nice.
Sometimes it is full of spice.
I like the color and the taste,
I won't let it go to waste.
But there are some things I'll never eat,
Like the eye of a newt or dragon's feet.

It's not my best poem, but at least it rhymes!

When we ate our lunch, my sandwich was having extra trouble travelling down my throat. I imagined myself as one of those **skinny snakes** that eats a whole egg without chewing it, and it goes down really awkwardly and slowly.

Daniel breathed his lunch in in less than a minute. I guess that's how he eats when he's nervous. Whereas Charlie smiled and nodded all the way through his lunch, as if he was reminding us and himself that it was going to be OK.

We went to meet Mrs Hutchinson after we'd

eaten and she walked us over to Mr McLeary's
office.

'Will you stay with us?' I asked.

'Yes, I'll stay with you,' said Mrs Hutchinson,
winking. Her heels were making

click -clack

noises and her hair was bouncing to the

rhythm. It made me sort of want to sproing

one of her curls to see what it would do. So I

shoved my hands in my pockets.

When we knocked, Mr McLeary said, 'Uh . . .

come in, we've just finished here.'

He was brushing crumbs off his jumper, but

they just landed on his trousers, which were

black, so I could see at least seven crumbs. He

must have been eating his lunch at the same

time as doing a head teacher telling-off routine, because a grumpy-looking kid from Year 3 was being marched out of the office by her teacher.

This seemed to turn Daniel's feet into

BLOCKS OF CEMENT

that he couldn't carry forward any more.

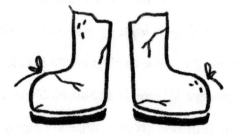

'Maybe I shouldn't come in . . .' he whispered.

I guess he was thinking of all the times he'd been sent in there as the naughty kid.

'It'll be fine,' I said, and gave his hand a squeeze. The squeeze seemed to melt his cement blocks, because we all ended up on chairs in front of Mr McScary's desk.

Mrs Hutchinson began to explain the whole fundraising project, while our hearts thudded in our chests. I could hear Daniel's and Charlie's . . . or was that just mine? I grabbed Charlie's hand under the table and squeezed it too. Charlie squeezed mine back. Mr McScary's lips were pulled in and pressed together really hard, as if he was trying to hide them. The only word he said so far was 'Uh-huh'.

Then I could hear Mrs Hutchinson saying,
'Go on, Omar, tell Mr McLeary what kind of
things you want to sell.'

My words were stuck in my head. I needed
to imagine my old pal H_2O. He's the

cool steam-breathing dragon

I used to imagine all the time when
I needed more confidence. Things had been
going so well lately that H_2O hadn't made an
appearance for a while. But I needed him now,
so I quickly thought of him swooping down with
a big dragon grin! He was holding cookies and
origami birds in his hands and then he started
juggling them.

I don't know how long it was that I didn't

speak for, but when Mrs Hutchinson said,

'Omar?', I was ready.

'Mr McLeary, thank you for listening to

our ideas. We would like to sell delicious

homemade cookies, origami birds made by my

friend Daniel here, and maybe our old toys and

books. It's probably best to set up a table to sell them at lunchtime or after school.'

Charlie and Daniel were staring at me as if they were thinking

WHOA, you Said it!

I was impressed by my own grown-up-ness.

Then Charlie sat up straight and said, 'Organic cookies!' with a big Charlie kind of smile.

Mr McLeary cleared his throat. *Here it comes*, I thought. *He's going to say something like*

ABSOLUTELY NOT, YOUNG MAN.

But then I got a huge surprise.

'Yes. Sure. Of course you can. I'm impressed. Great initiative, all of you. Well done.'

And then the weirdest thing happened . . . Mr McLeary's lips curled up into a

Smile.

He was smiling at us? Amazing!

I thought of H_2O's juggling and I realised what he was trying to tell me. Encouraged by the not-so-scary head teacher's smile, I blurted out,

'Talent Contest!'

Everyone looked at me.

'We're planning a talent contest to raise money, but we need a hall. What do you think about us having it in the school hall, Mr McLeary? We could even sell the things on the same day instead of at lunchtime.'

Mrs Hutchinson's curls perked up.

Charlie and Daniel were nodding their heads in agreement.

'Sure, why not?!' said Mr McLeary. 'That's really good thinking. I'll make arrangements.'

And he smiled again.

We filed out of his office and spent the rest of the day bouncing around with excitement, which was really good for after-school football club. Daniel scored six goals.

OH, YEAAAH!

Six goals was two more than Jayden, who is used to being the best goalscorer. But Jayden was a good sport, because he still high-fived Daniel at the end and Ellie gave him one of the keyrings that hung on her bag. (She still had sixteen of them left.)

When Mum picked me up, I didn't shut up about it all the way home and as soon as I got in, I ran upstairs to tell Maryam the great news.

But when I bounced into her room, she wasn't

alone. She had her friends over.

'OH MY GOD, OMAR.
YOU CAN'T JUST
BARGE INTO MY
ROOM WHENEVER
YOU LIKE!'

They were plotting ideas to fundraise for the

mosque. I looked down at their brainstorm, and

in bold across the top it said:

Objective:
Make more money than
Omar and his friends.

CHAPTER 11

I was on the phone to Charlie, and then to Daniel, right away. We couldn't believe Maryam's crafty plots!

'She's such a GIANT SNAKE-EATING LIZARD,' I said.

'Yeah, she's a HAIRY TOAD,' said Daniel.

'Charlie said she was an

ELEPHANT WITH ITS BOTTOM ON ITS FACE,'

I giggled.

And then we laughed so hard about our alternative swear words that we forgot all about how annoying Maryam was.

I guess it wasn't too bad anyway, because it meant more money for the mosque, but I still didn't want to lose. I wanted us to make way more money than Maryam and her friends ever could! After all, she was doing it for Silly and mean reasons, and we were actually doing it to save the mosque. Mum and Dad always say that the reason why you're doing something is super important, because you could be doing something good for the wrong reasons, like just getting people to say that you're ˌawesome. But even if you're doing something that you think isn't even that fantastic but it's for really great reasons, then that's better. I thought about that, and decided that Allah would be on our side. Though then I wondered if He would approve of taking sides . . . Well, if He did,

he'd be
on ours
for sure!

We knew we had to work really hard to make sure Maryam's gang didn't win. We spent every lunchtime and every break time, for the whole week, planning our talent contest and the things we'd sell. Mrs Hutchinson was helping us a lot. We chose her to be on the panel of judges, with Mr McLeary and the three of us. She also said that she'd see which of the school governors wanted to be on the panel too.

That Thursday, when we got the date from Mr McLeary for when we could use the hall, Mrs Hutchinson spoke to the whole school about it in assembly so that kids would know and could start to plan what their talent would be. Then she made Charlie, Daniel and me stand up, because we were the organisers.

'Sheeesh,' Daniel whispered,

'I feel so IMPORTANT.'

We all did. Especially because now that
everyone knew, kids kept coming up to us in
the playground to tell us or even show us what
their talents were. Like there was this Year 2
kid who knew the whole of Dr Seuss's *Green
Eggs and Ham* by heart and he literally went
through it without blinking. And there was
this other kid in Year 4 who could do a

BACK FLIP!

'Are we allowed to enter too?' asked Charlie.

'Hmmm, good question,' I said. 'I guess
we could, but we ARE the judges, so maybe it

wouldn't be fair . . .'

'What if me and Charlie entered and you were the judge, Omar?' said Daniel.

'Sure,' I said.

'Thank you, thank you, Sam-I-Am,' said Charlie with a grin. 'I'm going to do something with my double joints!'

'I'm going to sing!' said Daniel.

'WHAAAAAT?'

I'm not sure that Charlie and I are ever going to run out of surprises with Daniel as our friend.

I wondered what my talent could be. Once, my mum told me that my smile was so real and happy that I could make anyone do anything with it. I imagined performing this talent at the

contest, **HYPNOTISING** the

whole hall with my smile and then making them

do barmy things, like pat their heads and rub

their tummies at the same time while sticking

their tongues out. It would
be so funny. And then I
decided that if it worked on
Mr McLeary, I would super
definitely get him to change
the school dinners to

PIZZA and **CHIPS**

every day (except Fridays, of course, when it

would be fish 'n' chips!).

The best part was designing the tickets.

Mrs Hutchinson said that we could draw them and then the school would print them out and sell them to parents every day at home time.

Here's what we came up with (I did the bit with the kid juggling):

An evening of entertainment.
Come and watch our talent contest!

Prize: YOUR PICK—
an Oxford Dictionary
OR
a gumball machine!

Just £2 to enter the contest.
Tickets: £3
School Hall, Tuesday 18th, 7pm

OK, the prize isn't great, but we don't really have money to buy a better one and Mr McLeary kindly offered those. We're pretty sure N◉B☺DY will pick the dictionary, but we didn't feel like we could say that to Mr McLeary.

I couldn't wait for the weekend, when Charlie and Daniel would be coming round to make lots of stuff to sell on the day. But, as you might have guessed,

Miserable Madam Maryam almost ruined it all ...

CHAPTER 12

I know it's good to be **ambitious**.

Mum and Dad are always talking about it. But

Maryam and her friends took the ambitious

thing and went

loopy nuts with it.

On Saturday

morning, when I was lost in my Xbox games,

waiting for *my* friends to come over, Maryam

had invited *her* gang round. I only found

out when Daniel and Charlie rang the

doorbell. Maryam's friends were

taking up the whole of the kitchen table with their paint mess. (Mum only lets us paint in the kitchen where there's no carpet.) You won't believe this, but they were trying to paint pictures that they could sell for £500 each. They were doing it, even though (or maybe *because*) Mrs Rogers' son John is an artist and he says it's hard to sell art but when you do you can make a lot of money.

In fact, Mrs Rogers was sitting with them, telling them to make another splatter here and darken the tones there. She looked up and grinned at me with a cheeky face that I didn't even know grandmas could have. That face told me she knew Maryam couldn't sell any of those paintings for that much money and it was hilarious.

'DAAAAAAAAAD!'

I complained. 'Where are my friends and I going to make *our* stuff? We need the kitchen table too!'

'You can do yours tomorrow, brat face,' said Maryam.

Her friends giggled.

My friends grimaced.

'Tomorrow is Science Sunday, missy,' snapped Mum.

Esa picked up a paintbrush and started painting his own face, while Dad tried to figure out what to do.

118

Then Mrs Rogers said, 'You can use my kitchen.'

'Really?' said Dad. 'That won't be a problem? We don't want to be a bother.'

Seriously cheesy. . . my dad was too polite sometimes.

'We'll take it!' I said quickly, before Mrs Rogers changed her mind.

So Mrs Rogers and her kitchen were all ours for the day, which was super excellent because when we baked the cookies, she let us use her **mother's Secret recipe.**

'Mrs Rogers is old, so if this recipe is her mum's, that means it's from the proper olden days,' Daniel whispered as we sampled the first

batch.

Oh, Delicious Mother of all Biscuits!

We stopped and stared at each other. They

were out of this world.

We were going to make

some big bucks!

After we baked loads of cookies, we all helped Daniel make more origami birds, and then back at our own houses we chose some toys and books we had grown out of to sell.

I didn't have many, because I gave them away when I moved home, so I took a deep breath and put a couple of toys in that I still played with. It was hard work being **charitable** sometimes. I wished I had more things to sell. I couldn't stop thinking about what might happen if the mosque did shut down. Mum and Dad might not find their secret smiles in any other mosque and we'd all have to travel much further. Other people from the community wouldn't have a nearby place to pray and meet their friends either. And Mrs

Rogers wouldn't be able to come to the next

Eid celebration at the mosque like she wants to.

It made me feel all worried again thinking

about that, so I sent Allah a quick little prayer.

'Please, please
let the talent
contest go well.'

CHAPTER 13

At breakfast on Monday
morning Maryam said,
'Omar, shall I show
you where your room
is? It looks like you've
forgotten because

YOU KEEP COMING INTO MINE!' I gulped down
the spoonful

of porridge I had in my mouth and stared at

her, wondering what the big problem was.

'What are you staring at? Seriously. You came in the other day when I was with my friends and you even came in last night when I was sleeping, fumbling about like an amoeba brain!'

'What? Why would I—'

'I bet you were looking for things to sell at your stupid talent show.'

'Maryam!' Mum stepped in. 'That's quite enough rudeness from you. How dare you accuse Omar of swiping things from your room.'

'What? I don't believe it. You always take his side. HE'S THE ONE COMING INTO MY ROOM!'

Maryam gave up on her breakfast and folded her arms.

Dad said, 'It's quite all right for Omar to come into your room, you know. We don't treat family like strangers. And, after all, he's your dearest, darlingest, *only* brother – you never know when you might need to depend on each other.'

I giggled. And even Maryam giggled and quickly rose to the opportunity of pointing out Dad's mistake. 'What about Esa?'

'Oh yeah, I forgot we had him.'

Dad winked.

Esa turned over his bowl of Coco Pops in protest. That almost made us late. Almost.

There's nothing Mum and Dad hate more

than lateness. So even a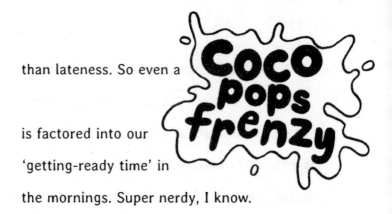

is factored into our

'getting-ready time' in

the mornings. Super nerdy, I know.

I knew the rest of the day was going to pass

sooooo slowly, because I absolutely couldn't

wait for talent contest day. By the time I got

into bed that evening, I felt like I'd lived

through a million hours, not just fourteen.

*

On Tuesday morning, as I was hopping into the

Peanut, my heart was racing. Talent contest day –

OH YEAAAH!

Mrs Rogers was in her driveway putting her rubbish in the dustbin. 'Omar, is your spa open today? I could do with a foot rub.'

'Not today, Mrs Rogers, but you can come to the talent contest,' I shouted back through the car window.

And then I thought about the fact that I hadn't ever seen her feet . . . What if they were covered in **fungus** and she had really long toenails because she's too old to bend over and cut them?

Ewwww!

I was **SUPER NERVOUS** all day.
Was it going to go well? Was it going to be a
big hit? What if nobody turned up to watch?
What if we didn't sell any cookies?

Charlie checked and double-checked and
triple-checked that we had everything ready
and in place for the evening. Charlie and Daniel
practised their talents, and basically so did the
whole rest of the playground.

The *Green Eggs and Ham* kid had added
cartwheels to his act and I could have sworn
Sarah was humming through the whole of
Maths and Citizenship.

When I went to the loo, I practised smiling
in the mirror, but it made me feel silly, so I
stopped. I wasn't entering the thing anyway,
so I didn't really need to worry about whether

a smile-hypnosis act would work. I focused on
how busy I'd be with the judging to help calm
my nerves.

In the evening Mum took me back to school
early to meet my friends and set up the hall.
The rest of the family, including Mrs Rogers,
were going to turn up with all the other guests.

I took my donation of toys and a big box of samosas that Mum had made and said we could sell at 50p each. They smelt so

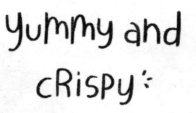

yummy and crispy.

that they made my tummy grumble and get confused about whether it was nervous or hungry. I shoved one into my mouth as we walked towards the hall.

When we got through the door, I spotted Mrs Hutchinson right away. She was talking to someone really tall who I'd never seen before. I walked over and that's the first time I met him . . .

Lancelot Macintosh.

'Ah, hello, Omar,' Mrs Hutchinson said. She turned to the man that she was talking to and said, 'This is the young boy I was telling you about.'

The man gave a little flourish-y bow and said to me, 'Lancelot Macintosh at your service! I'm the uncle. Your teacher's uncle that is. And luckily a school governor too, so I

have the honour of helping to judge the contest
with you this evening.' And he smiled a real
smile, the kind that makes your eyes smile too.
I wondered if he had an *actual* hypnosis smile,
because I liked him straight away! I liked his
weiRd moustachte – it was
the kind
you only see on French waiters in cartoons, all
curled up at the sides. Nobody *real* has that
kind of moustache. But Lancelot Macintosh did.
He smelled of bubblegum
and he was
holding a fancy walking stick that he didn't
seem to need at all. He was wearing a tweed
jacket and trousers that were too short for
him with bright red socks peeking out from
underneath. I wondered if it was because he

was so tall he couldn't find any to fit. And then he said,

'Yeessss. Marvellous. Marvellous,'

for no apparent reason.

A Year 3 teacher walked past in a hurry, sending her light-as-a-feather silk scarf gliding down to the floor, but Lancelot Macintosh spun round and caught it on his walking stick before it hit the ground. He wasn't even looking in her direction when it fell! SO cool! He plucked it off the stick and gave it to me.

He smiled. 'Why don't you return that to its owner?'

I did, and the teacher was so happy she put £5 in my donation box.

I went right back to Lancelot Macintosh, though, because he was so interesting. Daniel and Charlie had arrived and Lancelot Macintosh was telling them about a man who had been the Formula One World Champion THREE times, even though he was involved in a big accident. He'd just started answering all of the MILLION QUESTIONS we had about it when Mrs Hutchinson reminded us we had a big job to do. We all scurried off to finish setting up the chairs and putting up a banner on the stage – in just half an hour the show would be starting!

CHAPTER 14

The show went off with a BANG.

I mean, *really* it did, because one kid from Year 6 thought it would be cool to do a science experiment on the stage, and he must have put too much of something in, because it made a big scary noise and there was yucky stuff everywhere.

I sneaked a quick look at Mum and Dad, who had their proud and disappointed faces on at the same time. They were probably so excited about someone else loving science enough to do it as their talent and a bit gutted that he'd messed it up.

We saw handstands, ballet, singing, a bit more singing, poetry, taekwondo, acting, more singing, breakdancing, juggling and,

Oh, for the love of pancakes,

more singing!

Lancelot Macintosh clapped really loud for each kid and said, '*Marvellous!*' as if their talent was the best thing he had ever seen. Except for when the science went wrong, which is when he said, '*Ah, toads!*'

Sometimes his reactions were more fun to watch than the

talents themselves. I couldn't stop glancing at him. Every so often he would twiddle with his moustache, and twice he looked over at me and winked.

Then it was the interval, which is when everyone could walk around and buy the stuff we were selling. Everyone was talking about the cookies. They were the first to sell out, next were the samosas. Daniel's origami birds weren't doing so badly either. Lancelot Macintosh bought five. And he never leaned on his walking stick. Not once. I wondered why he even had it. It was like a prop. Maybe for tap dancing?

I thought he was probably full of mysterious surprises.

By the way, you might be wondering why I keep calling **LanceLot MACINtosh** by his full name. That's because he is one of those people whose name *has* to be said in full. You can't just call him Lancelot or Mr Macintosh. It doesn't sound right at all.

The talents after the interval were more exciting. *Green Eggs and Ham* kid came on. Somebody had cleverly attached a microphone to his jumper, so we could still hear him when he was upside down. I heard Mrs Hutchinson whispering happily along to some of the words.

Daniel and Charlie had decided to do an act together in the end, because Charlie had felt a bit too shy to do one on his own. Daniel sung a song by an old band called The Beatles

while Charlie did an awesome

ROBOT
DANCE

that made the

most of his weird

double-jointed elbows. They

looked like they were

having the most fun

ever, even

more than

the time they had a

competition to see who

could fit the most Maltesers

into their mouth!

Then a girl from Year 4 came on wearing

a Batman costume and did the best Batman

impression I've ever seen a kid

do, because kids have

SQUEAK

voices and Batman

does not. But that wasn't it! She had on a

Spider-Man costume underneath, and she hung

from the curtain as if she had sticky spider

fingers, then she had an Iron Man costume

under that! I couldn't believe all the voices she

could do.

Lancelot Macintosh loved this. He stood up

and said,

'Bravo!'

That was the final performance, so we

had a mini break while all the judges wrote

down their choices. I chose the last girl as the

winner, and *Green Eggs and Ham* kid as the
runner-up.

Mrs Hutchinson gathered together all our
slips of paper and her curls seemed to get

EXTRA BOUNCY

as she read them all. 'We picked exactly the
same winner and runner-up – it's unanimous!'

Then she went onto the stage to announce
the results, but first she said, 'We wouldn't
all be here today, if it wasn't for a young man
who hasn't performed but who has a great
talent of his own. Omar has shown great love,
compassion and drive. He cared greatly about
how it would affect others if our local mosque
were to close down – and he did something
about it! That, to me, is just as much of a talent

as standing on stage, Omar.

We are proud of you and of Charlie and Daniel.

Well done.'

For a minute I thought I felt a lump in my
throat. Nah, it must just have been the samosa
I had shoved in earlier . . .

CHAPTER 15

After the show, when everybody had left, Mrs
Hutchinson counted up the cash. The poor
caretaker, Mr Martin, started cleaning up all
the mess. There were a LOT of napkins and
cookie crumbs on the floor. Dad said we should
all give him a hand by putting
the chairs away, so we did.

Then Mrs Hutchinson and Mr McLeary came over to Mum and me, saying it was important to give me the cash straight away. Lancelot Macintosh referred to it as 'the day's takings'.

There was £ 1,419.50.

My shoulders

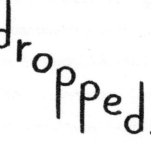

'Oh . . .' I said. 'That sounds like a long way off from £30,000.'

We'd worked so hard, for so long. Maybe making money wasn't as easy as I'd always thought it was.

'A marvellous amount, young boy!' said Lancelot Macintosh.

'You've done so well, Omar. You don't realise it, but that's a whole lot of money, and it's going to go a long way towards helping the mosque,' Dad chipped in.

'But it won't save it,' I said.

'Don't worry,' said Mum. 'Lots of other people are raising money too. I'm sure it will all add up to make up the amount they need.'

I looked at Maryam, remembering that her and her friends were trying too.

Mrs Hutchinson's curls looked sad for me. I didn't want them to be sad, so I gave my best smile and said, 'It's great! Thank you for your help, Mrs Hutchinson and Mr Macintosh. I'm going to keep thinking and come up with more ideas!'

I shoved the envelope of cash in
Mum's bag, and everyone got
back to putting the chairs
away. When I glanced up,
Lancelot Macintosh
was staring
into space
and twiddling
his moustache as if he was
thinking about something very deeply. Funny. I
wondered why.

Mum and Dad could not stop talking about
how proud they were of me on the way home.

Mrs Rogers said I was the

Best could-be grandson she ever had.

Maryam said nothing, but she did grunt every time someone else said something nice. I thought it would be kind to give Maryam some of the spotlight. After all, she had been working hard to sell her art for the mosque too. Also, I was curious to know if she was making enough to help save the mosque. So I said, 'How's your art stuff going, Maryam?'

Maryam looked a bit like Esa does when he's been caught drawing with Mum's lipstick. 'G-great. Great actually! I sold three pieces for £500 each.'

'Wow, that's amazing,' I said.

But Dad said, '*Did* you now?' In his *I'm-your-dad-and-I-know-when-you're-lying* voice.

'**YES!**' said Maryam.

'I DID!'

And then when Mum gave her an *it's-OK-love*

look, as we pulled into our drive, she practically

BURST
INTO
FLAMES.

She flung the car door open, and jumped out,

saying, 'Don't believe me then, you never do!'

We all gave each other the look we do when

Maryam acts like a complete teenager. Dad

followed her to her room to talk to her, and the

rest of us fell into our beds, exhausted.

Before I fell asleep, I thought about the cash

in Mum's purse. I imagined it

multiplying like bacteria

to get to £30,000. Yep, Mum and Dad even
love making us learn the yucky science stuff!
Bacteria can go from being just one of them
to hundreds of them in minutes. Imagine if
money could do that too . . . But I bet if
it did, Maryam would try to sneak it
away because she'd be so jealous.

CHAPTER 16

When I woke up the next morning to get ready for school, I thought I'd take a quick peek at the cash. Maybe Allah would have performed a miracle and it would *actually* have multiplied!

I went to get Mum's bag. But when I opened it, the envelope wasn't there.

'MUUUU

UUUUUM!'

I yelled.

'Did you put the money

somewhere else?'

'No,' said Mum. 'What is going on? Isn't it in there?'

'No. It's not.

Wherrrreeee issssssssss ittttttttt?'

I super panicked.

Dad came back into the house with his motorbike helmet on. He looked like an

ALIEN DAD.

'What's happening?'

'The money is gone!' I said.

'Such melodrama,' said Maryam, who was eating her breakfast already.

'I want pancakes,' said Esa.

Dad took off his helmet, as if he needed to scratch his head to think. 'Right. Maybe it dropped out at school? Or you didn't put it in the bag?'

'I did. I did.' I scratched my head too.

'Are you 100% certain?'

'Yes. Super certain. 500% certain!'

'Oh Allah,' said Mum.

Dad turned to her and said, 'Right, I'll go with him to the school and find out what's going on.' Then to me he said, 'Go and get your helmet, Omar.' Now I was thrilled and worried at the same time. I hardly EVER get to ride on Dad's bike with him. It felt

like I was in a movie and Dad and I were the

whizzing about to save the day. Hopefully . . .

We raced into school and Dad explained the whole situation to the school secretary. I tried to stand patiently while he did that, but I was feeling very IMpatient. Finally the secretary got everyone together. Mrs Hutchinson, Mr McLeary, Dad and I all searched the school hall super thoroughly. I was kind of sure it would come out from behind the curtains or inside one of the stacks of chairs, but when it didn't I started having trouble breathing.

'Let's check the corridors on the way out to the car park,' said Mr McLeary.

So there was still hope.

Nothing was there, though. I felt really panicky. *Where is it? How can it have just*

vanished?

There was still the car park. But as that was the last place to check, I was absolutely frantic and was finding it harder and harder to concentrate on searching.

It wasn't there either.

It was nowhere to be found.

At that point Mrs Hutchinson confirmed that she *had* seen me putting it in Mum's bag.

The conclusion?

The money had been

STOLEN.

Everyone was really worried. Mrs Hutchinson's hair was doing things I'd never seen it do before.

I was trying to be brave. I held onto my helmet, my hero-in-the-movies helmet. The hero wouldn't cry. I wouldn't either. I wouldn't. But then Dad took me into a hug, with all his leather motorbike gear and strong arms and dad smell underneath, and I cried.

I cried a lot.

CHAPTER 17

Charlie and Daniel were super upset when I told them about the money.

Daniel kicked a tree stump and then fell on the floor yelling out in pain.

'The tree didn't take the money!' I laughed.

'But someone did,' said Charlie. 'We can't let them get away with it.'

'Yeah!' said Daniel.

'Let's make a list of **SUSPECTS!**' said Charlie, excited. 'I mean, nobody knows the details better than we do.'

I perked up.

I loved this idea!

I got us started. 'OK. Who was around at the end, when Mrs Hutchinson gave me the money?'

'Us. Your parents. My parents. Daniel's parents. Mr Martin. Mrs Hutchinson, Mr McLeary, Lancelot Macintosh, Mrs Rogers and Maryam,' said Charlie.

Then we all started talking at once about who we thought did it.

We came up with a pretty good list of suspects and their reasons for doing it.

1. Mr Martin:

Was heard grumbling about cleaning the place up when nobody was near him. Something about *not getting paid enough for this nonsense.* Had a good chance to snatch the money because nobody was talking to him at the time.

Motive – disgruntled about not getting paid enough. Needs the money.

2. Maryam:

Has been jealous right from the start. Right meanie. She's super sneaky and quiet, so could easily have taken it.

Motive – to use the money to pretend she's sold some of her art, which she hasn't, and to destroy Omar's plans.

3. Lancelot Macintosh:

Nobody is that nice and cheery. In the movies it's always the nice guy, the one you don't suspect and that everyone likes, so it must be him.

Motive – he needs more money to replace the clothes in his wardrobe because they all shrunk in the wash (which is why his trousers are so short).

4. Mr McScary:

Maybe he really
is scary and was just
pretending to be nice so
he could spoil everything.

He's the head teacher, so he could stand near
Mum's bag without anyone thinking he was up
to something.

Motive – to make us pay. For what?
Errmmmm, for being kids. He hates kids.

We completely ruled out Mrs Hutchinson
and any of our parents. We debated about Mrs
Rogers. I know her the most and I was super
definitely 500% sure that it wasn't her, but
Daniel and Charlie insisted she had the best
chance to snatch it while she was in the car

with us. I didn't like it, but I added her onto the list.

5. Mrs Rogers:

Always full of
surprises and often has a
cheeky smile on her face.
Had a good chance to
snatch the money in the
car.

Motive – just for some entertainment because she's cheeky like that.

And just for the fun of it, and to make us feel a bit better, we imagined some out-of-this-world suspects too.

(6.) Mind Monster:

A mind monster had

stormed in and simply

taken the money right

before our very eyes,

but he controlled our minds so that we didn't

realise what was happening until the next day

when he was already halfway back to Zeyr, the

planet he came from.

Motive – the ruler of Zeyr needed the

money to plant trees, which they don't have on

their planet.

(7.) Invisible Man:

An invisible man had strolled in, dipped his hand in Mum's bag and taken the money without anyone seeing him.

Motive – he chose to use his invisibility for evil, rather than good. (Which, by the way, is the opposite of what I would do if I were invisible. I'd go and shut down factories that make too much pollution by flicking off their switches and leaving them wondering what happened.)

We decided to carefully investigate each of our suspects over the next few days.

'You live by Mrs Rogers and with Maryam, so

you'll have to cover them,' Daniel said to me.

'Uh-huh,' I said,

feeling a bit sick in my tummy.

'Don't worry, Daniel and I will work on Mr Martin and Mr McScary, and we can figure out how to get to Lancelot Macintosh together,' Charlie said.

'Thanks, guys,' I said, slumping my shoulders.

*

That whole evening Maryam was super annoying. She watched her

boring TV shows

instead of agreeing to play *Minecraft* with me.

I kept wondering if she did it or not – would

she really spoil things like that?

Over dinner, as I pushed my food around my plate because my tummy felt like it wasn't going to accept any food at all – like it was going to chuck anything I swallowed right back up and out of the mouth I dared to chew with – I said to Maryam, 'What do you think should happen to the person who stole the mosque money?'

Dad raised an eyebrow.

Maryam shrugged. 'I don't know. Go to prison probably. Right, Dad?'

Hmmmmm, quite a normal response. It was so hard to tell. And hard to figure out if she did it.

Dad said, 'I hope whoever it was gets caught, and if they do, the authorities will deal with them.'

Esa starting throwing his peas off his plate one by one.

'What on earth are you doing, Esa?' said Mum, jumping up.

'I can't eat those,' he said.

'They're not halal.'

We all exploded with laughter. Maryam sprayed juice all over herself and the table.

EWWWWW.

'Fruit and vegetables are always halal, dummy!' said Maryam, wiping herself off.

As she wiped her mouth, I thought about Lancelot Macintosh's moustache.

Was it some kind of disguise?

Why did he come to our talent contest? Could he make himself invisible?

CHAPTER 18

The next day, the most exciting thing happened during Literacy. Charlie was sent to get some photocopies of our worksheets and he came back all out of breath and wide-eyed with what looked like both FEAR and EXCITEMENT. It was sort of like the time he ate too many strawberry laces and went all hyperactive.

He sat down and said, 'I can't believe I'm still alive.

AAARRGH!

It was so fun but so terrifying.'

'What was? What did you do?' I whispered.

'Tell us,' said Daniel.

Charlie stood up again and then sat down again and then tried to look for his pencil before he finally blurted out,

'I broke into Mr McScary's office.'

'You? BROKE? You broke into . . .?' I managed.

'Whoooooaaaaa. Yes! Charlie!' said Daniel.

'OK, well, actually I didn't have to break in – the door was open. But I went in!!! I could see from the photocopy room that he wasn't

in there and I really didn't know when he might come back, but something in me just said DO IT and my legs started running without my brain giving permission!'

'What did you find?' I asked, still in shock.

'I was looking for the stolen money, but it wasn't there.'

'That doesn't mean that he didn't do it, does it? He might have spent it?'

'Yes, you're right, but I saw a copy of a letter

on his desk that he had written to the local

police station . . . and, well, he had written it to

talk about the missing money and said how upset

he was about the whole thing and he wants

them to do more to help us. And, well . . . I

might have taken the letter and it possibly

. . . *might* . . . could be in my pocket.'

Charlie breathed quickly in and out and

bounced on his chair.

'Never in a MILLION YEARS

would I have imagined you doing that, Charlie!

I'm rubbing off on you!' Daniel gave him a

proud slap on the back.

'Show us,' I squealed.

Charlie handed over the letter and we

passed it to each other secretly, ignoring nosey

glances from Ellie and Sarah.

'Yup. He's innocent,' I said.

'Innocent,' agreed Daniel.

'I feel like a SECRET AGENT or something.' Charlie looked down at his hands as if he couldn't quite believe what they'd done.

'You are, Charlie! That's one suspect down, four to go. We're like SUPER-SPIES.' My brain went into overdrive, trying to think of how we were going to investigate everyone else – how could three kids be more like James Bond?

Daniel had his thinking face on. 'I reckon I have a plan for Mr Martin . . .'

Charlie and I leaned in just as Mrs Hutchinson noticed that we weren't really concentrating on our worksheets.

'Boys, don't make me come over there to
find out what you're chatting about,' she said
in her voice that she uses to mean
I'm not cross but I will be in
approximately 47 seconds.

Super spying was going to have to wait.

*

At home that evening I couldn't work
out whether to think of money-
making ideas or spying ideas
– it made my head hurt! To
cheer myself up I imagined
H_2O trying to be a super-spy
and hide his huge dragon body
behind a tree, which made
me laugh out loud.

The deadline for the mosque building work was drawing closer and closer. We only had eight days left. I rummaged through my keepsakes box for inspiration, and found a painting Esa made me when he was two years old. It was in quite good condition and was of birds made out of his handprints in bright colours. I had kept it because it was so cute (don't tell anyone just how much I love him, OK?). I figured if it meant something to me, it might mean a lot to Dad.

So I went to look for Dad and found him in the garden pulling out some weeds, probably because Mum made him in exchange for her cooking the dinner today. Dad would never do gardening

just because he wanted to.

'Dad, will you buy this for

£5,000?' I showed him the card. 'Esa will

never have tiny hands like this ever again . . .'

Just then, Mrs Rogers popped her head over

the hedge and said, 'How's the money making

going?'

'That depends,' I answered.

'Dad? Was that a yes?'

'Erm, no.' Dad shook his head.

'It's going badly, Mrs Rogers,' I said.

But I laughed. I guess it had been a pretty

RiDiCULOUS

way to try to make some quick money. Dad and Mrs Rogers laughed too.

'You keep the painting, Omar – Esa made it especially for you. But I'll let you have £10 for helping me with the weeds,' said Dad, opening his wallet.

'Cool!' I said and stuck it in my jeans pocket.

'And we could make some more cookies for you to sell, Omar?' Mrs Rogers added kindly. 'I know they won't raise as much as the talent show, but every little helps, eh?'

Then and there I decided to cross Mrs

Rogers off our suspect list. There was just
NO WAY she'd taken the money –
she'd helped us loads, and she'd been really

looking forward to visiting the mosque with us

too.

Nope,
she definitely
didn't
deserve to be
on there.

CHAPTER 19

The next person we investigated was Mr Martin,

following Daniel's super-spy plan.

Daniel had decided we should watch

the caretaker's comings and goings every

lunchtime, so that we could set a

tHiEf TRAp. We started the day we

made our suspect list and his routine went like

clockwork. Every day at 1:20 he went to the old

shed building on the edge of our playground

to return the broom and mop he'd used in the morning. On Friday, we finally put our plan into action. I felt really wobbly – we only had a week until the mosque's deadline, and we still had no idea whether we would find the culprit.

At 1:15 Daniel quickly ran over to the building while Charlie and I kept watch. He left his Batman wallet just outside the shed door so  Mr Martin couldn't miss it. It had £5 in it too. Daniel knew this was a big risk, because he might not get his pocket money back, but he said he was happy to do it if we could find the thief.

Daniel ran back to us with his eyes all BIG LIKE SAUCERS and we all went to sit next to the big tree that would give us the best view of the shed without looking suspicious.

'So,' Charlie said, 'if he keeps the wallet, he's dishonest and he's probably the one who did it.'

'Exactly,' said Daniel, rubbing his hands

together and licking his lips. He was really

getting into this spying job!

Just a couple of minutes later, Mr Martin

appeared. For a second we thought he hadn't

seen the wallet and we all held our breaths

while we waited to see what he'd do.

Was our plan ruined? But when he'd

put the broom and the mop away he picked

it up, and looked around in a

Shifty way, like he was

searching for who could have

dropped it and whether they'd seen him take it.

We all made big eyes at each other:

THE PLAN
HAD WORKED!

But that afternoon in Maths, there was a knock on the door and Mr Martin came in looking really worried. He'd been going round to all the classes to ask if anyone had lost their wallet.

Daniel made a big show of being really relieved to have it back and said *thank you* about ten times.

For a second my tummy felt like it was scrunching itself up into a marble-sized ball, but Charlie squeezed my hand and whispered,

'Innocent.'

He was right. Maybe the trick had been worth it because now Mr Martin was officially off the suspect list. It didn't really make my tummy feel better, though, and all this ruling

out of people made me

EXTRA NERV☹US

because it made it more likely that it could be

Maryam. It did seem like she had a very strong

reason for doing it . . . I kept thinking of her

objective: **Make more money than Omar and his friends.**

I had to find out once and for all, so when

Maryam went for a shower that evening, I crept

into her room to look for the money. If she

had done it, the money would still be there,

because she wouldn't have been able to spend

it or donate it to the mosque fund without

causing suspicion.

I started with her chest of drawers, slowly

sliding each drawer open, really hoping not to

see a bunch of cash, and just then:

'OMMMMMAAAА

It was Maryam. She had come back to get
her special girly shower gel that she keeps in
her bedroom so we can't use it by accident.

'How dare you? This is the last straw!
You're such an annoying **brat**

and I'm telling Dad!' she threatened.

Then I did something that Maryam hadn't
expected me to do. And I hadn't really expected
me to do. I threw myself into her big sister
arms and cried.

'I'm sorry,' I sobbed through snot and tears.

AARRRRR!'

'I just had to see if you took it, because I'm desperate and I'm sad and I'm worried and my tummy won't stop hurting.'

Maryam hugged me back and told me to sit down. 'I would never do that to you, Omar . . . Yes, I do call you names and tease you and things. And **YES** you get on my nerves **ALL THE TIME** . . . but still, you're my *only* brother.'

That made us both laugh.

'Seriously,' she said. 'I would never actually do anything that made you sad for real. I promise.'

I believed her. Because her hug felt real and not even Maryam can lie *that* well. I gave her one more hug and crossed her off our list.

THE ~~CARETAKER~~

~~MARYAM~~

⬭ LANCELOT MACINTOSH ⬭

~~MR MASHABY~~

~~MRS ROGERS~~

~~MIND MONSTER~~

~~INVISIBLE MAN~~

CHAPTER 20

The countdown to the mosque's deadline felt like it was going faster and faster and faster the closer we got to it. We had managed to talk to all of our suspects except Lancelot Macintosh. But with just two days to go, and since we'd ruled everyone else out, we decided that he had to be the

'Should we tell the police?' said Charlie at lunchtime.

'They won't listen to a bunch of kids,' said Daniel.

'We have to try to lure him back into school,' I thought out loud. 'Maybe if we tell Mrs Hutchinson we really liked him, and we want him to visit our class, she'd ask him?'

'We did like him!' said Daniel and Charlie freakishly at the same time.

'I know . . . I really wish it wasn't him . . .' We liked him a lot. But maybe that's why we should be really suspicious of him, we decided. In movies it's NEVER the person you expect.

We did take our request to Mrs Hutchinson, who thought it would be a wonderful idea.

But she said that Lancelot Macintosh was an extremely busy man, so we'd probably have to wait at least a couple of weeks!

Even though we weren't going to be able to cross him off our list until it was too late to save the mosque, we couldn't stop talking about him, and all the things that were unusual and might make him a suspicious character:

'He smells of bubblegum when he's never even chewing. What is that about?'

'He holds a walking stick he doesn't use!'

'He really is too cheery.'

'He uses words that nobody else does. Ever.'

'His trousers are too short for him.'

I was super disappointed when Saturday morning rolled in. That meant zero days left to the deadline. Mum and Dad said that before the prayer the imam was going to be talking about how much money we had all raised.

The police hadn't found the missing money.

We hadn't talked to our prime suspect.

I don't think Maryam had sold any art.

There was no doubt about it:

the secret-smile mosque was going to shut down.

CLOSED

I was certain this would be the last time we went there. They were probably going to do a big goodbye because I hadn't been able to save it. **I couldn't breathe.** The air wasn't going into my lungs. I felt like I had suddenly been chucked onto another planet where breathing wasn't even a thing. I grabbed my neck in a panic.

I imagined H_2O blowing his cool steam towards my face. That made me breathe better. But I had to imagine him flying alongside the Peanut all the way to the mosque to stop getting in another panic . . .

PE 14 NUT

We took our shoes off and went in.

There was **pin-drop silence**.

I guess that's how it's supposed to be in

the mosque, but there's always some aunty

gossiping with another aunty, or some panicky

dad calling out his child's name because he

can't see her hiding behind one of the pillars.

We sat down on the soft carpet and watched

as the imam walked in.

But his shoulders weren't slumping and his

lips weren't turned down. They were curled up

into an unexpected smile. And his chest was

out, as if he was proud.

WHAAAAAT?'

Why would he be happy that the mosque had to close down?

Then he said, 'Dear brothers and sisters, children, neighbours and friends, I am so pleased to announce that we have *raised all the money* we needed to save the mosque. There have been many generous donations from all of you, and even young children have been going out in their communities to fundraise. Together we raised an amazing £25,000. But we still didn't think we would make it until we had an unexpected donation last week of a whopping £5,000 from a complete stranger – a Mr Lancelot Macintosh.'

WHAAAAAT?'

I practically choked on my own saliva. I couldn't believe it. What? Whaaaaat? Lancelot Macintosh? Our prime suspect? What the Batman bananas was this? Where did he get £5,000 from? He couldn't even buy himself some trousers that fit him, so why did he give money to the mosque? Nothing made sense.

CHAPTER 21

Mum and Dad were as flabbergasted as I was. They didn't have the answers to my questions either. But one thing was for sure: their secret smiles were as sparkly as ever. In fact, I had never seen so many teeth on display at the mosque before.

Yellow ones, white ones, missing ones, crooked ones, perfect ones, braced ones and even gold ones. All in the most

GINORMOUS
Smiles.

I couldn't WAIT to get into school and ask Mrs Hutchinson what was going on.

When we got home, I found a shiny pound coin on the ground in the driveway which I decided was an extra piece of luck. I snatched it up quickly before Maryam saw it and shoved it into my jeans. That's when I felt the £10 note Dad had given me for weeding. I had completely forgotten to donate it at the mosque, so I shot upstairs to my secret underwear hiding place to keep it safe.

I put my hand right to the back of the wardrobe to fish out my green underpants, but something was different.

'WHAT THE BUS ?!!'

The envelope of cash from the talent contest was there! With all the money. Every bit of it.

OHHHHHH MYYYYYY GODDDDDD!

I screamed all the way back down the stairs, tripped over my own foot and crawl-hopped through the hallway into the kitchen where everyone was.

'I found the money!'

Mum and Dad looked extremely confused. 'It was in my secret hiding place.'

'Wow. That's. Wow. *Alhamdulilah*,' said Mum,
which basically means 'thank Allah'.

'Who else knows about the hiding place?'
asked Dad, scratching his head again.

'Nobody. Just me.'

'That's a mystery . . .' said Dad. 'So weird.'

'Wait!' shouted Maryam, and darted up the
stairs at the speed of light.

'What's got into her now?' said Mum.

She came back with her phone in her hand.
'Look, look. This explains *everything*.'

Maryam unlocked her phone and brought up a video on the screen. It was a video of me. Or was it a zOMbie? Well, at least I looked as if I was the star of some sort of zombie show. I didn't have blood all over my face or anything but I was definitely different than usual. Maryam was saying things to me, but I was just walking around like I couldn't hear her.

'I recorded this after the talent show, when Omar came into my room AGAIN. But I was so sleepy, I forgot all about it, and I only just remembered,' said Maryam. 'Now, look carefully at his hand. He's holding a white envelope!'

We all looked up from the phone at each other's faces.

'He sleepwalks!'

finished Maryam. 'He moved the money when he was sleepwalking!'

Dad laughed. 'Wow. And this whole time we were going nuts thinking someone had stolen it.'

I opened my mouth wide like a shocked emoji.

'Why do you think you hid it, Omar?' asked Maryam.

'Well, I was thinking about the money before I slept and that you'd be really jealous about it—'

For that I got a whack on the arm from Maryam. And Maryam got an eyeballing from Dad. Then Maryam got a pinch on the arm from me and *I* got an eyeballing from Dad.

Then Esa said,

'I want pancakes!'

And Mum decided it was time to cook lunch.

By the time food was on the table we'd stopped being shocked and found it hilarious instead. I couldn't wait to tell Charlie and Daniel, and give the money to the mosque. We giggled about it for the rest of the day. *Poor Lancelot Macintosh*, I thought, *he never should have been a suspect at all.* And it turned out

THE MOST SUPER OF SUPER-SPIES WAS Maryam,

not me or Daniel or Charlie! I guess she's not such a bad big sister after all . . .

SECRET AGENT

AGENT # : 001
NAME   : MARYAM

CHAPTER 22

I practically flew into school on Monday

morning and when I skidded into the classroom

I saw him sitting there on Mrs Hutchinson's

chair. Walking stick in hand. Trousers too short.

Lancelot MAcintosh!

I pounced on him with the biggest hug ever

and didn't let go until Mrs

Hutchinson started asking why

I was stuck to

her uncle like a baby koala

Lancelot Macintosh had come in to talk to the class, just like we'd asked him to when he was our prime suspect. And you won't believe this: we found out that Lancelot Macintosh is super rich. He's practically a GaZiLLiONaiRe.

When he was a 'young lad' he had invented a small thingamajig that has gone into all cars ever built since then.

He told us all about it, saying 'marvellous, marvellous' every other sentence, and twiddling his moustache at least twenty times.

'So what do you do now, Mr Lancelot Macintosh?' asked Sarah. 'Do you just sit around and count your money?'

Lancelot Macintosh laughed a real hearty laugh. 'Well, I keep myself very busy trying to invent new things. Some serious things and some things just for the fun of it!'

Yup, it turns out that Lancelot Macintosh spends a lot of time trying to invent new flavours of bubblegum in his house. That explains a lot!

When he was leaving, he said quietly to me, 'Omar, you remind me of myself when I was a young chap. You really impressed me with your marvellous attitude. It reminded me of the days when I chased my dreams and

DIDN'T GIVE UP ON A THING.'

'Thanks! Is that why you gave the money to the mosque?' I asked.

'Yes, because I want you to believe in yourself and never forget the community that will be there to support you while you're chasing your dreams.'

I beamed.

Then he chuckled and said, 'Either that or something about that big smile of yours must have made me do it.'

No way, I thought.

My hypnosis smile!

I guess it works after all!

Charlie and Daniel threw me their *OHHHH, WOWWWW* looks.

*

At home, when I filled Mum and Dad in about Lancelot Macintosh, they were really impressed. Dad was even familiar with the *thingamajig* that he invented and couldn't believe he had met someone that had contributed to his driving experience so much.

Even Maryam seemed in good spirits, talking about how she loved his moustache style. 'It's so hipster,' she said, like she even knows what that means.

Mrs Rogers was over for a cup of tea, and she said, 'I could sew him some trousers to fit, you know.'

'I bet he could pay to sew him some trousers that fit with all that money,' laughed Mum.

The Queen

'I think he wears them like that on purpose,' I said. 'And I like him just the way he is.'

*

That evening, the doorbell rang. I thought it was another of Mum's online orders, but it was

Daniel and Charlie.

WHAAAAAT?'

I didn't know they were coming!

'*I* invited them, turnip nose,' said Maryam. But she said it sweetly somehow, as if she was using the funny cussing in an affectionate way.

'Why would *you* invite them??!' I asked.

'Well, I did sell one piece of art,' she said. 'To Dad!'

'Soooooo?' I was still super confused.

'Well, I didn't give the money to the mosque.'

'You called us here to tell us that?' said Daniel.

'OKKKKKK,' said Charlie.

'Not exactly . . .' Maryam was enjoying this so much.

'Come on, Maryam, stop being weird!' I pleaded.

She giggled. 'Follow me then!'

We all ran up the stairs behind her. In her room she had three wrapped presents on her bed.

'For you three,' she said, pointing.

We jumped on them like they were going to vanish if we didn't open them in three seconds.

WOWZERS!

WHOA! WHOA! WHOA!

Maryam had bought us the

LASER NERF BLASTERS

that we wanted with the money she had raised.

'Well, you do have *panda breath* but I'm kind of *proud of you*,' she said.

I pounced on her with a big hug. Then Charlie joined us and Daniel got super excited and jumped on us too.

CHAPTER 23

I don't know why, but whenever something unusual happens in my life, we seem to end up with biryani on our dinner table. Mum and Dad invited Lancelot Macintosh round for dinner to thank him for what he did for the mosque. Mrs Hutchinson was coming too, since he was her uncle and she'd helped so much with the talent show.

That day, Mum and Dad fussed around in the kitchen more than usual and tidied and cleaned until their backs hurt, because a gazillionaire had never been to our home before and they were nervous.

'What are you making, Mummy?' asked Esa.

'We're making biryani, spinach curry, naan, samosas, lassi and moussaka.'

'Mufasa? From *The Lion King*?' said Esa.

Mum giggled and explained that moussaka was an Arabic dish made with aubergines and minced meat and not Simba's dad from *The Lion King*.

'Remember when he used to call rice "mice"?' said Maryam, and then doing a squeaky impression of him she said, 'I want curry and mice for dinner.'

While we were in the middle of practically wetting ourselves with laughter, I heard the roar of an engine and I ran to look out of the window. There was a bright yellow Ferrari!

Oh Nutella in a Cake Ball!

For a minute I thought Allah had finally sent my reward for the fast I kept in Ramadan. But then I saw Lancelot Macintosh and Mrs Hutchinson hop out.

He is too cool !!!

I guess gazillionaires have lots of money and people with lots of money can buy expensive nice cars. And it's just like him to go for the most fun colour of all.

What happened next was better than anything in the ENTIRE Universe.

Can you guess? I got to go for a ride with him before we had dinner! Sure, he didn't let me drive it, even though I offered to pay him the £10 from my secret money hiding place, but, still, it was the Best TIME Ever!

ZANIB MIAN grew up in London and still lives there today. She was a science teacher for a few years after leaving university but, right from when she was a little girl, her passion was writing stories and poetry. She has released lots of picture books with the independent publisher Sweet Apple Publishers, but the *Planet Omar* series is the first time she's written for older readers.

NASAYA MAFARIDIK is based in Indonesia. Self-taught, she has a passion for books and bright, colourful stationery.